08/13
12.99

A Note to Parents

Your child is beginning the lifelong adventure of reading! And with the **World of Reading** program, you can be sure that he or she is receiving the encouragement needed to become a confident, independent reader. This program is specially designed to encourage your child to enjoy reading at every level by combining exciting, easy-to-read stories featuring favorite characters with colorful art that brings the magic to life.

The **World of Reading** program is divided into four levels so that children at any stage can enjoy a successful reading experience:

Reader-in-Training
Pre-K–Kindergarten

Picture reading and word repetition for children who are getting ready to read.

Beginner Reader
Pre-K–Grade 1

Simple stories and easy-to-sound-out words for children who are just learning to read.

Junior Reader
Kindergarten–Grade 2

Slightly longer stories and more varied sentences perfect for children who are reading with the help of a parent.

Super Reader
Grade 1–Grade 3

Encourages independent reading with rich story lines and wide vocabulary that's right for children who are reading on their own.

Learning to read is a once-in-a-lifetime adventure, and with **World of Reading**, the journey is just beginning!

Printed in the United States of America
First Edition
10 9 8 7 6 5 4 3 2 1
G658-7729-4-13001
Library of Congress Control Number: 20122942010

ISBN 978-1-4231-4813-5

World of Reading

Boogie Down

Adapted by Kristen Depken
Based on the series created by Dan Povenmire & Jeff "Swampy" Marsh

Disney PRESS
New York

It was a special day in Danville. The famous television show *Let's All Dance Until We're Sick* had come to town. They were looking for new dance contestants!

“They’re taping here in Danville!” Candace told her crush, Jeremy. “I’ve already entered us!” Candace was sure they would win the top prize.

But Jeremy didn’t look very happy. “I’m going to get some fresh air,” he said.

Jeremy went to the backyard. Phineas and Ferb were there.

Jeremy said he was worried about the dance show.

“What’s the problem?” asked Phineas.

“I don’t want to let Candace down,” Jeremy said. He didn’t think he was a good dancer.

"Maybe Ferb can teach you!" Phineas said.

Ferb wiggled his arms.

He kicked his legs.

He jumped and did a split.

"There's no way I can learn that by tonight," Jeremy said.

"Maybe you don't have to," Phineas replied. He had an idea that could help Jeremy. "Ferb, I know what we're going to do today!"

Then Phineas looked around the yard. "Hey, I wonder where Perry is," he said.

Phineas and Ferb didn't know that their pet platypus, Perry, was really a spy called Agent P! Perry was in his hidden lair. It was time for him to start another mission.

Agent P's boss, Major Monogram, told him the plan. The evil scientist Dr. Doofenshmirtz was up to something. He had bought all the potatoes, bacon, and green onions in the Tri-State Area.

"It sounds like a recipe for evil," Major Monogram said. "So get cooking, Agent P!"

Agent P zoomed off to Dr. Doofenshmirtz's headquarters. But the moment he got there, he was caught in a trap!

"Well, well, well." Dr. Doofenshmirtz laughed. "Look who's here—Perry the Platypus. All shackled up and no place to go."

The doctor and his robot, Norm, had used all the potatoes, bacon, and onions to make a big bucket of potato salad.

"I'm off to our annual evil potluck and press conference," he said. Then he aimed a laser at Agent P. "I'll just leave you here to meet your doom."

Dr. Doofenshmirtz and Norm left with the potato salad.

The laser beam moved toward Agent P. He had to get away quickly!

Fortunately, Dr. Doofenshmirtz wasn't very good at making traps. Agent P easily slipped his arms out of the metal cuffs. Next, he pulled out his legs.

Then he jumped up and ran after Dr. Doofenshmirtz.

Back at home, Phineas and Ferb had built a machine called the Ferbulistic Groove-a-Tron 9000. It looked like a metal skeleton.

"You put it on under your clothes," Phineas explained.

As long as Jeremy wore it, he could copy any dance move Ferb did.

The boys decided to give it a try.

Ferb raised his arms . . . and so did Jeremy.

Ferb did a disco pose. Jeremy did, too!

"Sweet!" Jeremy exclaimed. He was ready to go with Candace to the dance show.

Meanwhile, Dr. Doofenshmirtz met up with some other scientists. They were members of a new evil club.

Dr. Doofenshmirtz had invited all the reporters in town to the meeting, too. He wanted everyone to know about the club's evil plans.

There was just one problem. None of the reporters showed up! They were all at the dance contest.

"If the press won't come to us, we'll go to the press!" Dr. Doofenshmirtz exclaimed. "To the dance hall!"

At the hall, the dance contest had already started.

"Attention, citizens of Danville!" Dr. Doofenshmirtz yelled.

But no one even looked at him. Jeremy, Candace, and all the other contestants were too busy dancing.

The scientists realized that the cameras were all focused on the best dancers.

"Split up and start dancing like you've never danced before," the evil doctor told his friends. "Whoever gets on camera first could deliver our message of evil."

The evil scientists started to boogie. But they were terrible!

Dr. Doofenshmirtz and another scientist named Rodney were upset.

Dr. Doofenshmirtz covered his eyes. "Oh, the humanity!" he cried.

Rodney snorted. He thought he could dance better than everyone else. “This looks like a job for—” he started to say.

“Can it, Rodney!” Dr. Doofenshmirtz snapped. “We both know that I’m a better dancer than you. See you on the dance floor!”

Just then, Agent P arrived at the contest. Major Monogram sent him an urgent message on his radio wristwatch.

"You must stop Doofenshmirtz and his group of scientists before they broadcast their message of evil and interrupt what has quickly become my favorite show," Major Monogram ordered.

Agent P didn't have any time to lose.

On the dance floor, Candace and Jeremy were having a great time.

Suddenly, one of the judges pointed at another pair of dancers.

BZZZZ! The spotlight on those dancers went dark. They were out of the contest!

“Let’s kick it up a notch,” Candace said to Jeremy.

Backstage, Phineas and Ferb looked out from behind the curtain. Ferb gave Jeremy a thumbs-up. It was time to put the Ferbulistic Groove-a-Tron 9000 to the test!

Ferb wiggled his arms. He shrugged his shoulders. He got groovy.

The dancing machine under Jeremy's clothes helped him do exactly the same moves.

Dr. Doofenshmirtz tried to get on camera, too. He danced as hard as he could.

"You may begin quaking in fear," he said into the camera.

BZZZZ!

His spotlight went out. The evil scientist was eliminated.

Rodney also gave it a try. "Hello, my future subjects," he said as he danced.

BZZZ!

His spotlight went out, too.

Across the stage, Jeremy's dancing was amazing, thanks to Ferb. First he twirled Candace. Then he dipped her close to the floor.

"Wow, Jeremy. You are really good!" Candace cried.

"Bravo!" Candace's friend, Stacy, called from the audience. "Go, Candace!"

Stacy threw a bunch of flowers to Candace. They landed in the middle of the dance floor.

A bee came out of the flowers. It buzzed over to Ferb! He swatted at the bee. But it kept flying in his face.

Because of the dancing machine, Jeremy started swatting the air, too! Fortunately, everyone in the audience thought it was a great new dance move. They all waved their hands in front of their faces.

Up above the stage, Agent P sprang into action. He tossed a cloth down.

It landed on an evil scientist.

Then Agent P threw his hat.

It knocked over some paint cans.
They also fell onto the evil scientists!

Dr. Doofenshmirtz was getting desperate. He started pushing dancers out of their spotlights. But Rodney had the same idea.

"If anyone's pushing this dancer out of the way, it's me!" Dr. Doofenshmirtz cried.

"I was here first!" Rodney shouted back.

The evil scientists battled over the spotlight. It almost looked as if they were dancing together.

Dr. Doofenshmirtz sighed. "This is awkward," he said.

At that moment, Agent P soared above the dance floor.

Wham! He knocked into a disco ball.

The disco ball crashed right on top of Rodney and Dr. Doofenshmirtz! Agent P's mission was a success. He had stopped the scientists from broadcasting their message of evil.

The thud from the disco ball knocked Jeremy to center stage. He was the only dancer left. It was time for Ferb's best moves!

With the machine's help, Jeremy danced so quickly that his feet became a blur. He ended in a split. The crowd went wild!

"I see quite a future for someone with moves like that! " the contest host exclaimed. "How would you like to dance until you're sick every week?"

"Do it, Jeremy!" Candace cried. "We could be stars. Dancing stars!"

But Jeremy shook his head. He felt guilty about taking credit for Ferb's dancing.

He pulled the Ferbulistic Groove-a-Tron 9000 out of his clothes. "It was this doing all those dance moves," he explained.

Everyone gasped.

Then Jeremy pulled the curtain back to reveal Ferb.

"Well, it looks like my work here is done," Ferb said.

He danced offstage.

The judges gave Ferb a perfect score.

“I’m sorry, Candace,” Jeremy said. “I didn’t want to let you down.”

Candace smiled. “I just wanted you to come out with me and have a good time,” she said. “You know, dance until we’re sick.”

“Well, I am feeling a little dizzy,” Jeremy replied.

Candace put her arm around him. “I’ve got you,” she said.

Candace and Jeremy walked home. It had been an exciting day. With Phineas and Ferb's help, Jeremy had really boogied down.

And he was pretty sure that he had done enough dancing to last him a lifetime!